THE TIME HACKERS

Also by Gary Paulsen

GARY PAULSEN

THE

TIME

HACKERS

WENDY
LAMB
BOOKS

Published by
Wendy Lamb Books
an imprint of
Random House Children's Books
a division of Random House, Inc.
New York

Wendy Lamb Books is a trademark of Random House, Inc.

Visit us on the Web! www.randomhouse.com/kids
Educators and librarians, for a variety of teaching tools, visit us at
www.randomhouse.com/teachers

Library of Congress Cataloging-in-Publication Data

Paulsen, Gary.
The time hackers / Gary Paulsen.
p. cm.
Summary: When someone uses futuristic technology to play pranks on twelve-year-old
Dorso Clayman, he and his best friend set off on a supposedly impossible journey
through space and time trying to stop the gamesters who are endangering the universe.
ISBN 0-385-74659-8 (trade) — ISBN 0-385-90896-2 (library binding) [1. Space and
time—Fiction. 2. Computer games—Fiction. 3. Science fiction.] I. Title.
PZ7.P2843Ti 2005
[Fic]—dc22
2004006634

The text of this book is set in 12-point Goudy.

Book design by Michelle Gengaro

Printed in the United States of America

January 2005

10 9 8 7 6 5 4 3

BVG

To Paul Bowering, for his humor

CHAPTER ONE

He should have known better and opened his locker more slowly. Some sense should have warned him. There were enough strange things going on; he should be more cautious.

But no. No, he had to come bombing down the hallway and work the last number on the combo on the door and jerk it open without thinking.

There was an adult male hanging inside. Dead. Not only that, but it was a medical cadaver, partially cut open with long pins holding things in. And not only that, but it was an *old* cadaver.

Runny.

And the stink—Oh, my, he thought, only in different words. Much different words. Oh, my, the stink was positively alive, rolled out in a semigreen cloud, and he could hear flies coming inside from out in the schoolyard, zooming to the odor. Oh, yes, there would be flies. Of course flies. And they would stay around. Last time when he found seven hundred and twenty-one and one-half dead lab rats in his locker, packed in tightly, the flies had stayed for a month even when the rats were gone.

It was a joke. Some joke.

Dorso Clayman held his breath and closed the locker door, looked up and down the hallway to see if anybody was watching. Nobody seemed to be paying special attention but that didn't mean much. Someone might have a small camera on him, getting his reaction on a digit-disk to broadcast later. He decided to play it nonchalant. Cool. As if he *always* had bodies in his locker.

And it would have worked except that Susan Racher walked down the hall at that moment, right past his locker, and the smell drifting, no, slithering out of the bottom grill on the locker door dropped her cold. Literally. She went down on her knees, grabbing for her inhaler. Susan was one of those who always acted sick but never actually was. But then she keeled over onto her side, one leg jerking feebly. For a second Dorso did nothing. Susan was always faking it.

But this time it seemed real enough—her eyes had rolled back and were showing only white. So he grabbed her by the wrists and dragged her down the hallway past the smell zone. He propped her up against the wall and put her inhaler in her mouth.

"She dead?"

Dorso looked up to see his best friend, Frank Tate, look-ing down at Susan. "She's going to miss her first class if she's dead," Frank said. "They don't like it if you miss homeroom even if you're dead."

Dorso shook his head. "No. She's just out for a little bit. The smell caught her wrong."

"What smell?" Frank sniffed. "Is there something stinking?"

"You're kidding . . . ," Dorso started, then remembered that Frank had a sinus condition that kept him from smelling things. Frank had once run his bicycle over a dead skunk on the highway without noticing it, even though part of the skunk had stuck to a tire and kept flopping around and around as he rode, the stink blowing up in his face with each rotation. Bulletproof, Dorso thought, a bulletproof nose. "I had a body in my locker."

"Again? Man, don't they ever think of anything else to do to you? Last time they put a dead dog in there, and then there were the lab rats, and of course the time they stuck in the six or seven thousand dead frogs . . ."

"This time it was human. Some medical student's job, it must have been. But old. Really old."

Frank nodded. "Yeah. It would have to be old. That's how it works, isn't it? You can't transport anything current and the system won't go into the future, so it has to come from the past." As he talked he went to Dorso's locker and grabbed the handle. "How did it look?" He jerked the door open.

"Don't—" Dorso started, but then he shrugged. It had been more than thirty seconds, and none of the . . . surprises . . . ever seemed to last longer than half a minute.

"It's gone," Frank said. "Too bad. I might have recognized it from when I did all those medical research scans for my anatomy study."

"You were just looking for naked pictures."

"Still. It's research, isn't it? And at first it wasn't a protected zone. If the government didn't want you to see it they would have put the blocks on the way they did with religion and later with naked pictures."

Dorso left Susan and moved back to his locker. The

smell was still almost as strong as it had been when he'd first opened the door, but the body was gone, all traces of it, even the stains. Well, that was good, at least. He held his breath and took out his gym bag. He had gym first period, which was a stupid time to have PE, but he was stuck with it if he wanted to take computer science second period, which he had to do because Karen Bemis took computer science then and he thought if he could be around her enough she might begin to notice him. It hadn't happened in two years but he still had hopes.

His gym bag reeked of the dead body. That meant the smell had gotten into his gym shorts and T-shirt as well.

Great. I'll stink like a cadaver. Just great.

He looked down the hallway where Susan was getting to her feet, her eyes dazed as she leaned against the wall, and for about the ten thousandth time that month he thought maybe it had been a bad idea when the scientists had figured out how to crack time.

CHAPTER TWO

It was strange how it had happened, Dorso thought, walking slowly toward the gym, hoping the stench would dissipate before he got there.

Some lab technician in Texas had fired one electron through a linear accelerator near the speed of light onto a receptor plate, where there were hits from two electrons, and when they were trying to figure out where the second electron came from they found a way to go back in time and bring traces of the past forward.

Sort of.

Of course, it didn't happen quite that fast. At first all that the scientists could bring forward were fuzzy images, almost impossible to see, and there was no way to control what they would get. They could jump into the past and project images onto a screen in the present, but they couldn't pick the time or the place, and for the first year it amounted to little more than a very interesting technotrick. They might see a vision of a dinosaur one time and on the second try get an image of a man who might be Julius Caesar getting ready for a bath, or Anne Boleyn getting her head chopped off.

Initially only the supercomputer labs could make it work, because it required a warping of the time line that took loads of electrical energy.

But then they found that the new Super Chip developed by Roger Hemmesvedt in his basement in Fort Garland, Texas, made it possible for anybody with a personal computer to play with the time line. That blew *everything* wide open. The chip not only provided access for everybody, but when its output was coupled with a built-in clock, it let you pick the time you went to. If you used data from GPS equipment it became easier to pick the place as well.

Soon people going to work on trains were able to access the time line and get pictures on their laptops of Shakespeare writing, or the Battle of Gettysburg, or Jesus actually giving the Sermon on the Mount.

In the beginning there were amazing effects. Many of the more money-oriented evangelical ministers found themselves going broke when people listened to Jesus directly instead of needing a middleman. History teachers had to actually study history and know the facts. They couldn't just be football coaches killing time until the season started.

Of course, there were problems. Initially there were no controls on subject access, and for a time there were naked pictures of Cleopatra in her bath and Helen of Troy standing nude in a window frame all *over* the place. It was an exciting time to study history.

But the tech wizards soon invented the sliding chip block, so all the new Super Chips could block out anything offensive to the viewer—or what censors and auditors might think was offensive. There were constant court battles to decide what young people should be able to see.

Then they discovered the hologram projector chip, which allowed anybody with a laptop not only to pull images from the past but also to project them anywhere they wanted, and for a short period it was impossible to drive down a road without seeing some historical image on a wall or some figure from the past standing in a yard.

Finally someone discovered how to bring smells forward with the image, and that nearly put an end to the freedom of access everyone had come to enjoy, because the scientists were worried that if the smell came, perhaps viruses would come as well, and what would happen if somebody brought a plague victim forward into a city and the plague got loose?

But only the smell came, no solid bodies, and while no one could quite understand why that was, there were no bacteria, or even viruses, introduced from the past. In the end, that was that.

But no one could see into the future for the simple reason that it hadn't happened yet, and there were apparently no other split dimensions or alternate time lines to find. Nobody had invented antigravity boots or a skateboard that flew or ray guns that blasted people to bits (unless you counted the lasers the military was using) or ships that went to the stars.

At least not yet.

There was, Dorso thought, entering the gym, just this messy time line business and the normal humdrum life that he had going for himself, with no blips on the horizon except that somebody, somewhere, had decided to make him the recipient of a string of strange techno-practical jokes.

Bodies and dead rats and frogs had started appearing in his locker about three months earlier; then it got positively weird. There would be images mixed with other images—a carp stuck halfway through a pane of glass, alive and wiggling; a Brazilian soccer player looking normal except that his bottom half was a tricycle; and a dog riding a bicycle upside down.

None of it made sense. Dorso didn't have any real enemies unless you counted the entire football team, who seemed to think he was some kind of toy and were constantly playing catch with him, throwing him up in the air or stuffing him into containers. But they did that with most of the boys who didn't play football, except for Waymon Peers, who at thirteen was six foot four, weighed two hundred and fourteen pounds with no fat, and told them he'd pinch the head off the first player who messed with him. The team didn't seem to single Dorso out. Besides, he was sure none of them were smart enough to turn a laptop on, let alone go through the complicated process of acquiring a time line, projecting it backward to access an image, and then projecting the image forward in a hologram. It wasn't that the process was very difficult, but it was beyond most of the players, who sometimes seemed to take days to learn their locker combinations.

Dorso's life had gone on in spite of the practical jokes, which weren't really much of a bother except for the smell, and he'd come to almost expect them. He was walking down the hallway carrying his laptop, which contained all of the material in the textbooks, when an image of George Armstrong Custer appeared next to him.

One of the byproducts of time projection was that everybody knew what all the important people in history looked like. Cleopatra really wasn't all that pretty, Shakespeare had bad teeth (of course so did everybody else back then, but Shakespeare had the surprising habit of picking at his with his pen and he always had ink on his lower lip), and John Wilkes Booth, who killed Lincoln, looked and acted like a drugged ferret.

Dorso knew instantly that it was Custer, who was dressed in the buckskins he wore the day he was killed in the big battle. Dorso had watched the battle several times, so seeing Custer wasn't that surprising. He was standing with his side to Dorso, looking away. He had a Colt revolver in his hand, and as Dorso watched—the image was only apparent for thirty seconds—Custer turned toward him.

That was when something happened that bothered Dorso. A lot. Dorso had seen many images, historical events, and famous people brought forward, and the same rule always applied. The paradox of time was called the grandfather rule. It said that you couldn't go back in time physically or affect time, because if that could happen you could go back and kill your own ancestor, and that would mean you wouldn't be able to exist to go back and kill your own ancestor, and so it couldn't be possible. The physics of time would not allow you to change time. Period. You could not affect time; therefore, people or events from the past could be viewed but never altered. The people being viewed could never know they were being seen.

And that had always been the case for Dorso. Whatever he'd seen and done, the subjects had never been aware of him.

But now, as Custer turned, for a half a beat his eyes looked confused, as if he didn't know what was happening to him, and he looked directly at Dorso, *into* Dorso's eyes.

Dorso blinked. He had to be wrong. But no—Custer looked right at him, into his eyes, and had started to raise his hand when he was hit by a bullet and fell to one knee and then down on his side as the hologram faded.

CHAPTER THREE

"Custer looked at you?" Frank liked new things, different things, liked it when things out of the ordinary happened, but he was skeptical. "You mean his eyes just turned toward you. It was the battle, right? He was very busy. I've watched the battle several times, trying to get a good look at Crazy Horse. There are no pictures of him, you know. He wouldn't allow it. And the tech censors threw a block on him because they felt he would want it that way. So you can't get a good picture of him. But I know that he came up over the back of the hill and might even have been the man who shot Custer, and I thought the blocking committee might have missed him because they wouldn't know he was there but I was wrong—"

"No." Dorso shook his head. They were sitting on his front porch. Dorso's parents both worked, and he and his six-year-old sister, Darling (yes, that was really her name, and as far as Dorso was concerned she was about as darling as a wolverine, and twice as destructive), were latchkey kids. Dorso watched her each evening until his parents came home, and it was a full-time job. Right now she was chasing the neighbors' cat across the yard, holding a doll dress in one hand and a teacup on the other. She periodically tried to dress the cat in doll clothes and make it sit at tea parties or picnics. The cat didn't like it. At all.

"Custer looked at me. He saw me. He was bewildered and he looked into my eyes. . . ."

"Not *into* them," Frank said. "*At* them. Or in the general direction of them. And of course he was bewildered. He had just made the biggest mistake of his life, and every Native American in the world was about to ride over him and they were *mad* . . . boy, were they mad. But he couldn't have looked at you. Not really— Oh, look, she caught the cat. She's dressing him. I think that might be the record. Usually the cat makes it harder. Remember last time how he took her up that elm in the backyard and across the clothesline before she caught him on top of Emerson's Buick? The cat must be getting old. Or else he's giving up. . . ."

"Frank, quit changing the subject. I'm having a problem here and I need your help."

Frank turned from Darling back to Dorso. "You don't have a problem, you just *think* you do. You're imagining things. Come on, you know the time paradox as well as me. You can't go back and change time because it could make you not be here."

Dorso nodded but then shook his head. "No, wait. We just *think* we can't mess with time. But how do we know that?"

"Because they figured it out, that's why."

"Who?"

"What do you mean, 'who'?"

"Who told us that?"

"Scientists, math guys, people who play with numbers. The time freaks. The same goons who put in all the time blocks so we couldn't look at naked wom—so we couldn't study anatomy. That's who."

"But what— Darling don't unscrew the cat's head that way, it'll come off. What if they're wrong?"

"The time freaks?"

"Sure. Look, all this is new. Maybe they think you can't go back and change time, but all these theories have been just that, theories. Nobody ever thought we'd be able to go back and look at Jesus preaching the Sermon on the Mount, but now we can."

"Yeah. It's great. And who thought He'd turn out to be that color?"

"I'm just saying what if all those guys are wrong and somebody has figured out how to go back and mess with time?"

"Look at that! I never would have guessed you could tie a knot in a cat's tail that way to tuck it up under the dress. And look at him just sitting there. Isn't that cute?"

"It's because he's terrified. Last time she gave him a bath when he fought her. He really doesn't like the whole bath thing. The soap hurt his eyes and he smelled like bubble bath for a month and the alley cat that comes through once a month on his rounds thought he was a sissy and cleaned his clock and you're changing the subject again."

"Because you're nuts, Dorso. Let's try to look at what you're saying in a rational way."

"When," Dorso asked, "have you ever been rational?"

"This isn't about me. It's about you. And what you're

trying to say is that someone, somewhere, some genius who is smarter than anybody in the whole world has ever been, someone with the giant intellect it would take to conquer the time paradox has done it, and is using it—get this now—is using it to play practical jokes on a twelve-year-old kid. Is that what you're really saying?"

"Well, when you put it that way . . ."

"And you call *me* irrational?"

Dorso studied his sister on the lawn for a moment. The cat was sitting quietly in the doll dress at a little table, looking across the table at Darling as if waiting for a cup of tea and a scone. I wonder, Dorso thought, if a cat would eat a scone, and what is a scone? "Still, there's something weird going on."

"I think what's weird is you. You're imagining things and making them real in your mind."

"I'm not imagining the body in my locker or all the dead frogs, and I'm not imagining Custer looking at me either. He looked right into my eyes."

Frank shook his head. "And through you, out the other side. He was looking through you at all the Indians coming down on him, and that's *all* it was. You've got to relax. I tell you what—this weekend let's have a history marathon. We'll go back and see all the battles of the Civil War—not the whole battles, just the high spots; all the charges . . ."

But Dorso wasn't listening. It didn't matter what Frank thought or said; there was definitely something very strange happening, and he couldn't help thinking that it wasn't over yet.

CHAPTER FOUR

His name was Ludwig van Beethoven. In his own opinion, he was the greatest composer who had ever lived and indeed might be the greatest who ever would live.

And he was angry.

Of course, if you spoke to anybody who knew him, knew of him, had ever met him or had even been in the same room with him, you would find that he was always angry.

Indeed, he sometimes thought anger was the force that drove him.

And right now he was furious. He made his way through the streets of Vienna on foot—on his feet and not in a coach, by all that was holy!—to tutor an addlebrained young girl who didn't know the first thing about music, simply because he was almost penniless again and her father was rich enough to pay hand-somely for her to hammer away at a pianoforte while Ludwig pretended to teach her.

Stupid! Not the girl, all of it. Well, he thought, the girl too.

And for nothing. Time wasted, life wasted, thought wasted and all for nothing except a few coins when he should be in the middle of his own music.

He turned a corner to take a shortcut, trying not to break into a run, and stopped dead.

Ahead of him the alley turned into a long, dark tunnel, stretching away to nothing, to a point of darkness. My mind, he thought, my mind is going.

Worse, in front of the tunnel, staring at Beethoven with his mouth open, was a young boy dressed in outlandish clothes and strange shoes, carrying a small tablet of some kind.

It did not last long. The boy jumped back, then stretched out a hand as if to touch him, but Ludwig lashed out at the hand with his arm and swore and turned away just as the tunnel changed into a white light and the boy disappeared.

All madness, Ludwig thought; all is madness. Is this the way art treats us? Drives us mad? To see such things in the daylight?

He was shaken, so upset that he decided not to use the shortcut but to avoid the boy and the tunnel and go a longer way. He hadn't taken five steps when he came upon an old man stumbling down the side of the road.

"Out of the way!" Beethoven cried, but the old man did not hear, and when Beethoven moved to brush past him he saw that the man had a sign hanging about his neck and was holding a cup.

I AM DEAF, the sign proclaimed. But it was nothing to Beethoven, because many were deaf then. First they suffered from an affliction so painful that it caused them to pull at their ears. Eventually, they went deaf. It was nothing. Only people of the street were affected; so far no one in the upper classes had become ill. The disease only took the very poor and uneducated.

But as Beethoven brushed past him the old man coughed and sneezed and filled the air with hundreds of millions of viruses that nobody knew existed, would not know about for decades.

Several thousand of them floated into the air in front of Ludwig and into his open eyes, where they found a ready home in the moisture, and from there traveled to his bloodstream, where they stayed until they could move to his ears and cause the infection that, in three years, would lead to Beethoven's complete deafness. Beethoven, who called himself the greatest composer in history.

CHAPTER FIVE

Frank shook his head. "I still think you're missing a chip or two."

They were walking near the library on a bright, warm Saturday morning. Neither of Dorso's parents was at work that weekend, so he didn't have to watch his little sister. He wanted to use the mainframe computer at the library to download some history data for a paper he was doing on early American train wrecks. He could get the data from the Internet, but sometimes the lines were so busy he couldn't get through. The library kept several infrared entry ports open all the time for visitors, and they were almost always available. The best part of working at the library directly with the mainframe was that it was so fast. And it got him away from Darling for a bit. She was studying ambush techniques used in jungle warfare—or so it seemed to both Dorso and the cat—and had almost caught Dorso in a punji pit filled with tigers earlier that morning, if you could imagine the cat as a bunch of tigers in a pit. Dorso had to admit that the job she had done on the cat with poster paint did make him look like a tiger, albeit a small one.

"My laptop is fine. I ran a diagnostic and—"

"I mean in your head. You said Beethoven saw you and ran off."

"He took a swing at me, Frank! He took a swing at me and *then* he ran off down this alley. He saw me and got this scared look in his eyes and then he said something in a foreign language—I think he was swearing at me—and then he took a cut at me and then he ran off."

"Then the UFO came down and beamed you up out of there and they got you on the spacecraft and took a long copper wire, which they inserted in your—"

"Frank! Be serious about this. I'm telling you this is really happening."

"Or you think it is."

"What does that mean? You think I'm crazy? That I'm hallucinating all this?"

"Well . . ." Frank shrugged. "I *had* thought about that, but I think there's a more logical explanation. Look, what have you got so far? Some yack is playing practical jokes on you in some way we don't quite understand, and you saw Custer right when he saw all the angry Native Americans in the world and he seemed to look at you and then you saw Beethoven and he seemed to look at you . . ."

"No." Dorso shook his head. "He *did* look at me."

"But what if he didn't? What if he was looking past you or through where you were standing at somebody who was getting ready to mug him? You said it was in an alley, right? Maybe he was about to get attacked and you and I both know Custer had plenty to look at right then. Think about it. What I said before still holds. Would somebody who has somehow managed to defeat the time paradox use it to play jokes on a kid?"

Dorso sighed. "I guess maybe you're right. Still, I wish this whole thing would stop."

"Let's do like I said before. We'll find some potato chips and pop and other junk food and have a historic battle marathon. Speaking of that, isn't it strange that they put the sliding chip blocks on naked women, which you would only study for art, of course, and yet they'll let you watch battles where guys are getting hacked and blown to pieces? Not that I want them to block out the battles, that would be just wrong, but what could it hurt to see Marie Antoinette taking a bath? Just for anatomical study purposes, you understand. Of course, my research tells me that apparently she never bathed. . . ." He stopped and nodded, thinking. "Hmmm. Maybe if we searched in the mainframe for the history of bathing, just looked for famous baths . . ."

He was going to say more, although Dorso wasn't listening because he'd heard it all before. Frank stopped and stared ahead of him and upward. He was looking directly into the rear end of a woolly mammoth. It had just pulled up a bunch of grass with its stubby trunk and was bringing it up to its mouth.

"What?" Frank stopped dead. Dorso, who'd been looking behind him because he'd heard a car backfire, took one more step and actually bumped into one of the mammoth's legs.

The skin felt coarse and was covered with thick hairs so bristly they almost scraped him. For half a second Dorso, struck by curiosity, stretched out a hand to touch the skin again and then he, Frank and the mammoth all came to the same conclusion at the same time.

Dorso shouldn't be able to feel the mammoth. Not if it was a hologram. He should be able to walk right through it. The mammoth felt much the same, that Dorso shouldn't be touching it, and it turned to its left and saw Frank standing there, openmouthed.

Just the day before, a somewhat similar biped, covered with animal skins and filthy hair, had tried to poke the mammoth with a sharpened stick. Now the creature dropped its grass and with some irritation reached back with its trunk, took Frank by the ankle and flipped him onto the library lawn in a spiraling throw that brought Frank skidding into a perfect three-point landing—nose, elbows and knees— directly in front of a KEEP OFF THE GRASS sign.

Then the mammoth vanished.

"All right," Frank said, his voice muffled as he spit out dirt and grass. "All right, you've got my attention."

CHAPTER SIX

"I'm thinking . . ." Dorso sighed. He seemed to be doing a lot of sighing lately. Better that than the hysterical screaming he ought to be doing. A live woolly mammoth. Good lord, what if it had come when he was somewhere else, say in a bathroom? Say it had come when he was sitting on the toilet, and it had filled the whole bathroom with woolly mammoth? How would he ever have explained that to his parents?

They were back in his room, where Frank was dabbing disinfectant on his scrapes and scratches.

"I'm thinking there's so much wrong with all this that we ought to go to the authorities," Dorso said.

"All right." Frank nodded, putting the disinfectant down and wiping his hands on a paper towel. "That's one way to approach it. The authorities would probably want to know about this, would probably want to know that somebody has found a way around the grandfather rule and has the potential to change the past and the future and could actually destroy the whole human race. Or . . ."

"Or? That's not enough? There's an 'or'?" Dorso frowned. "Although I think that might be a bit strong. Destroy the whole *species*? How could they do that?"

Frank looked at Dorso with pity. "Simple. Go back to where it starts and stop it. Drop a dime on Adam, you know, whoever or whatever Adam was, and bingo, scratch the human race."

"But then we wouldn't be here . . . the grandfather rule would kick in and they couldn't do it because they wouldn't be there to— Did you say 'Drop a dime on Adam'? Did you actually say that?"

"And there's your 'or.' "

"I beg your pardon?"

"We could tell the authorities, or . . ."

"Or what?"

"Or we could *not* tell them and try to figure this all out by ourselves."

"Are you out of your mind? You just saw a real woolly mammoth—not a hologram but a *real* one—that was brought forward in flesh and blood from the past. It picked you up and skipped you like a stone. This has gone way beyond our ability to figure things out. . . . Why are you shaking your head?"

"Dorso, Dorso, Dorso—my poor boy. You're missing the obvious."

"I am?"

"Sure. The truth is, this is the first time in the history of the human race that this thing has happened. Heck, *nobody* can figure it out. We can not figure it out as well as anybody can not figure it out, and we have the advantage that it's happening to you. Well, to *us* now, since I was the one the mammoth picked up. It's happening to *us*."

Dorso sat staring at his friend and was horrified to find

himself not saying anything. This was insane. This was the time paradox. The thing that all science said was impossible, the thing that could ruin it all, destroy everything. To not tell the authorities was insane. Yet he was silent.

"And there's the other thing," Frank said.

Dorso waited. Waited for the other thing.

"Well, two other things, really."

Dorso waited for the two other things.

"First, think of the opportunities to learn. We can see how time, how the core of all we are, how *time* works. If we can see how they do this and survive, whoever is doing it, we can bend and warp things. We can be rich. Think, we could go back and invest in Microsoft when it first started so our parents could be rich before we were born. We could be popular and good-looking . . ."

"How could we be good-looking?"

Frank shrugged. "I'm not sure, but if we know how to change time I'm sure we can work it out. The thing is, along with these other people we seem to be the only ones who know about this. What a chance. Money, power, knowledge— all of that to two twelve-year-old kids."

"Still . . . ," Dorso began, but he knew he was sunk. It was too much, too tempting. The idea of being rich, popular, maybe good-looking. Rich. "Still . . ." Then he shook his head.

"You said there were two things. What was the other thing?"

"Well, I'm thinking that if we can work this all out it will put us way outside the normal operating parameters for time viewing, give us some new angles."

"Sure. So?"

"I should be able to work around the sliding blocks and get some really good studies going. Maybe Helen of Troy, Nefertiti—the really classic ones."

"Ah, yes." Dorso nodded. "The naked ladies."

"Anatomical studies," Frank said. "Anatomical studies."

"Of course."

CHAPTER SEVEN

Six days passed.

Six long days in which nothing at all happened. That is to say nothing new.

The weekend roared through, Dorso's parents went back to work, school resumed, class fed into class. There was a moment of excitement when the history teacher said that no matter what they saw in time holograms, kids wouldn't understand history unless a teacher guided them through the controversy. Frank asked what controversy the teacher meant and the teacher said that all history was open to interpretation and Frank said there wouldn't be any problem at all if they would remove the blocks so that kids could see it all and not a watered-down version.

Life went on. The cat found a new hiding place by crawling through a small hole under the stairs and working his claws up into a floor joist to hang inverted like a sleeping bat. But Darling found that the vacuum-cleaner hose would just fit through the hole. She put the control dial on super-tornado-dust-atomizer-seventy-four and the cat came out nearly voluntarily and not totally bald.

So life went on, but it wasn't that Dorso and Frank

weren't working on the problem. Frank used his personal computer to do what he called logic flowcharts.

"Look, this is how I see it." Frank propped the flex-screen up against the wall. Their personal portable computers were little more than a flexible screen less than an eighth of an inch thick that could be folded or rolled up for storage. With built-in solar charging, there was no need for plug-in power, and with all data taken and sent through infrared data ports, there was no need for wires or hookups for modems. The computers had touch-sensitive keyboards implanted in the screen in such a way that they could be stored electronically in the data chips when not needed. Of course, with voice-controlled systems coded to operate only with the owner's voice, there was little need for a keyboard.

Standing in front of the screen as though he was making a presentation, Frank said, "Tell me if this is roughly correct. This has been going on for about three months, right?"

Dorso nodded, looking at the screen. Frank had made graphs and bar and pie charts.

"Okay, we'll call each event an incident. This line here is the incident-appearance line, coupled with this bar, which represents the height or depth or maybe the best word would be seriousness of the incident."

Oh, good, Dorso thought. An incident-appearance line coupled with an incident-seriousness bar. My life in graphs. If we could just work in a geekness-quantity pie chart my world would be complete.

"So they started kind of light, just weird images and holograms, little jokes—"

"If," Dorso interrupted, "you can call four cubic feet of dead and rotten earthworms jammed in your locker a little joke."

"Right. I know that at the time the subject considered these things serious, but we must have a logic base to start from. Initially, they were almost harmless pranks—"

"If," Dorso said, interrupting again, "you consider four hundred and thirty-one pounds of rhino excrement jammed in my locker a harmless prank—and did you just call me the subject?"

Frank nodded. "We have to keep it neutral to keep it accurate."

"I don't want to be neutral. I don't want to be a subject."

"We're getting off track here."

"Well, it's my track and I'll get off it if I want to and I don't want to be called the subject."

"How about calling you Subject Number One."

"No."

"What do you want to be called?"

"Dorso."

Frank seemed about to argue and then nodded. "Dorso. But let's get back to the charts. It started slowly, with silly prank holograms in your locker, isn't that right?"

"If you can call cadavers and dead frogs and lab rats silly pranks . . ."

"All *right*! So they weren't pranks. Still, they started at this lower level and then they got worse, isn't that right?"

Dorso frowned, remembering. He nodded. "Yes."

"So describe how they got worse."

"Well, initially they were just like you said—warped, weird little things, sometimes all mixed up, like they had two and sometimes three holograms combined by mistake. Or maybe on purpose. There was the ancient Greek athlete who had a headlight for a face, and Michelangelo's statue of David, only it was made out of green Jell-O with those small marshmallows and bits of fruit in it. Joke stuff. Then it went to disgusting things—dead bodies and squashed frogs and different loads of animal dung and then, finally, the scenes with Custer and Beethoven, where I know they saw me."

"But they were still holograms, right?"

Dorso nodded. "As far as I could tell. Now that I think of it there was lots of dust and noise with Custer at the battle but it disappeared when the hologram faded. And with Beethoven I think I would have felt his hand when he hit me. . . ."

Frank turned to the side and whispered into the computer: "Subject says severity increased with each incident."

"Frank."

"I'm sorry. *Dorso* says severity increased with each incident."

"And that's it, right?" Dorso looked at the charts and graphs. "That's all we know, isn't it? Which is nothing, really. Just that all these things have happened."

"No. Two more things." Frank held up two fingers. "One, the mammoth. That was an amazing new step. Now it's become real. Somehow they brought a live woolly mammoth from the past and dropped it in front of you. Think if it had been that way when they brought Custer—there would have been bullets and arrows all over you. Or if I hadn't sacrificed myself to the mammoth—"

"Sacrificed yourself?"

"I put myself in harm's way to protect you and the mammoth took me instead of turning on you. What if I hadn't done that?"

Dorso decided to let it go.

"Maybe he would have stomped on you," Frank said, "that's what. I mean, this has escalated to where it's life threatening. . . ." He trailed off, thinking.

"Two things," Dorso reminded him. "You said there were two things. You always say that. What's the other one—something to do with naked ladies again?"

"No." Frank pointed at Dorso. "We have to figure out why it's happening to you. Why not me, why not somebody else? What makes you the receiver?"

For a long time they sat in silence. Dorso tried to think of what might make him the target for these pranks, if that was what they were, and that made him think of himself, his life, who might hate him. He kept coming up blank. Born twelve years earlier; nice, ordinary parents who worked hard and were loving and fair; insane younger sister but insane in a good way, unless you were a cat she wanted to dress up. Got average grades; didn't do anything that would make anybody particularly upset with him; had only one emotional entanglement—Karen Bemis, who didn't know he was alive, or at least didn't show it.

There was just nothing about him that should draw this kind of attention. He shook his head, looking at the charts on Frank's flex-screen. He was about to say they should chuck it all and go to the authorities when something popped into his brain.

A word, there was a word bothering him. Something he'd said—no, something Frank had said. Something about how he was the target. No. Something else.

"Receiver." That was it. "What did you say about me being the receiver?"

"Just that—what makes you the receiver?"

"Yeah. That. The word made me think of something else. *I* can't really be a receiver, not in the technical sense. It would have to be a device. What if I'm not the target at all? What if it's something else and I just happen to be close to it?"

"But what . . . ," Frank started, then stared at his flex-screen. "Your laptop! You think it might be your laptop?"

Dorso rubbed his forehead, thinking. "Let's look at it. I never see the holograms unless my laptop is there, and every time one comes to my locker, it's been when I go to PE."

"And you leave your laptop in your locker. . . ."

"Exactly! There it is. My laptop is the target, not me. Somehow whoever is doing this is locking onto my laptop." Dorso had been carrying his computer rolled up and he brought it out. The computer came on automatically.

"But you leave it turned off in your locker, right?" Frank pointed to his own computer. "I turn mine off when I store it."

Dorso shook his head. "But with light and solar power they never really turn off. See, it's just the display and working circuitry that shut down. The internal workings, all the memory chips stay on all the time, so it can retain its programs.

Frank whistled. "That's it—it makes sense. There's just one more question."

"Always two questions?"

"Yeah—what does your laptop have against you? Or more to the point, since I'm the one who got flipped by the mammoth, what does it have against me?"

CHAPTER EIGHT

At precisely 7:47 the next morning, while Dorso's mother was back in the kitchen and Darling was dressing the cat as a G.I. Joe commando trooper who was having trouble keeping his helmet on straight and his weapons belt on correctly and who had no idea at all what he was supposed to do with his little plastic assault rifle, Dorso and Frank left to join a pirate ship and sail the Spanish main.

All unintentionally.

It happened in this way:

Frank had come to get Dorso to go to school. He had just knocked on the door and Dorso had opened it and taken a step outside, had turned to wave goodbye to his mother when there was a flash of white light and he tripped and stumbled against Frank. The two of them fell onto the deck of a sailing ship.

The sun was bright in a brilliant blue sky above a stunning blue ocean. In normal circumstances, the ship they fell on would have been beautiful, with its towering masts and gray-white sails. But what the boys fell into was war. Men who were almost unbelievably dirty, covered with clothing in rags and carrying axes and short swords, were screaming and swearing as they ran back and forth, while a short distance away another ship, bigger and much neater- and cleaner-looking, disappeared in a cloud of gray smoke as it fired off a broadside.

"Duck!" Frank screamed. Dorso turned and fell as a man who barely qualified as human took a swing at his head with a boarding axe.

"Blast!" he yelled. He raised his axe for another swing just as a cannonball from the other ship took out his center in a splash of something Dorso hoped he would forget.

"They come! They're boarding us!" someone screamed over the noise, and Dorso took a quick look around and saw that this was not the first salvo the ship had taken. Wreckage was everywhere, hanging from the yards and masts; boards were splintered and there were blood and chunks of flesh all over everything.

He saw a black flag flying from the stern.

"It's a pirate ship!" he yelled to Frank. "We're on a pirate ship . . ."

Frank was pounded from the rear by a falling slab of wood, so that he slammed into Dorso and drove him back and down beneath a board just as the other ship careened into them. Its men threw lines with boarding hooks that caught the pirate ship. Men came screaming over the side and into the remaining pirates with boarding axes and cutlasses, hacking and slashing and continuing the killing even when the pirates tried to surrender, throwing them into the water, where the blood had drawn sharks that quickly finished off any pirates who still lived.

It was over in three minutes. The men from the attacking boat stood wiping their blades on the rags of sails.

"Here's two more!" A man with one eye and a scar down the side of his face found the boys. "They ain't but sprites, sir, and they be dressed all queer. What do we do with them?"

"Sprites make brutes, Williams," a man in a blue uniform said. "Cut their throats and throw them over the side. Our orders were to kill them all."

"No, wait!" Dorso yelled. Frank was still groggy from being hit by the falling yard, and Dorso pulled him up. "We're not pirates! We're visitors from . . . no, we're captives. They took us captive and were holding us for ransom." Somewhere, Dorso thought, he'd read about pirates and ransom. Somewhere. Oh, yeah, *Huckleberry Finn*. "We're not pirates at all. . . ."

"A good story." The man in uniform must have been an officer in the English navy because he spoke very correct English. "Not very likely. Still, we should examine the situation before we go further. Why are you wearing such outlandish clothes? And those shoes. What are they made of?"

Dorso looked down at his sneakers and then at the bare feet of all the other men. "It's a kind of plastic. . . ."

"And what is plastic?"

"A kind of rubber." Frank shook his head to clear it. He pushed Dorso's hand away and stood alone. "From the rubber tree."

"Rubber." The officer frowned. "I don't know this

substance. What of those packs on your backs? Take them off and let us examine the contents. There's much here that makes no sense."

And that's when Dorso saw it, or rather him. On the other ship, but close, looking across at Dorso in complete shock. A young man, perhaps in his late teens or early twenties, was standing there, and he was staring at Dorso almost as if he recognized him, or at least knew that he was drastically out of place—or better yet, out of time. The young man looked down and seemed to jab at something Dorso just caught sight of before there was another blinding white flash and Dorso and Frank were back on the step of his house, waving goodbye to his mother as if only a hundredth of a second had gone by.

Except that both boys were splattered with spots of blood and wood splinters and had torn their shirts.

"Dorso?" His mother stared. "What on earth . . ."

"Oh," Dorso said, thinking fast, "it's all right. Frank had a nosebleed. You know, he gets them all the time. We'll clean off with the hose." He closed the door and dragged Frank around to the hose connection by the garage.

"Well," Frank said, sputtering as the water from the hose hit his face. "That was fun. . . ."

"We'll go in and get clean T-shirts for school and then we'll go to work on this."

"What? What is it? What did you see?"

"I saw a guy back on the English ship. He looked at me."

"Oh, great. You mean like Custer and Beethoven looked at you?"

Dorso shook his head. "No. He knew we were out of place and he looked surprised, really surprised. Then he looked down and jabbed something and we were back here."

"What do you mean, he jabbed something?"

"It was a keyboard," Dorso said, smiling. "I saw the corner of it. He must have hit the Escape key or something and ended the scene in some way. He was carrying a laptop."

CHAPTER NINE

"This is impossible." Frank stood in front of his locker.

Dorso nodded. "He's trying to cheat the time paradox."

"Not only that." Frank shook his head. "The rest of it."

"What rest of it?"

"Life. Here we are, on the edge of the greatest discovery of all time . . ."

"Or disaster."

"Whatever. Here we are, on the edge of the single biggest thing that's ever happened, and life, my dull life, goes on and on. I'm going to flunk a math test this afternoon and I can't tell anybody that it's because I was whumped by a mammoth and kidnapped on a pirate ship."

"You're going to flunk math because you didn't study, which is the same reason you *always* flunk math and have to take the tests over."

"That's it exactly! Here I am, with maybe the most perfect excuse of my life, and I can't tell anybody."

"Well, we *could* tell somebody else. We could tell the government. Or Mr. Cather, the science teacher. Or our parents. Which brings up something I didn't think of before."

"Right." Frank nodded. "If we tell somebody else we'll

lose our edge. You know. We might be able to use this to find treasure or see—"

"Naked women."

"Aren't you even *curious* about how Helen of Troy or other famous babes looked without any clothes on? And I started thinking that I might be able to go back and maybe *be* there. . . ."

Dorso stared at him, wondering for the thousandth time what made Frank tick. Or whirr. Or buzz. Or whatever it was he did inside that brain. "No. Not that. I was thinking how odd it is that nobody else has seen any of this."

"It's just us," Frank said. "It's aimed at us somehow."

"You ran into a mammoth's butt. A whole mammoth. And he picked you up and flipped you onto the library lawn. And nobody, not a soul, saw it? And we had half a navy on my front step and my mother didn't see anything? That's just crazy. I mean, it probably is my laptop, or it seems like that's the way it works. But why *my* laptop, why us? What did *we* do? And why can't anybody else see it?"

"Well, if we go back to my logic flow charts we might find—"

Dorso shook his head. "Nope. No more of me being the subject."

"Then all we've got left is your laptop. What did you do to it?"

"What do you mean? I haven't done anything to it."

"You must have," Frank said. "Why doesn't it happen to me, on my laptop? Just yours, right? So why?"

"I've never touched it. Besides, you know you can't mess

with them. It takes special tools and equipment . . ." Dorso trailed off, then reached into his locker and took out the laptop.

"What? What is it? You thought of something."

"Four months ago, or five, I had that problem, remember? It kept doubling the holograms. I'd see two of everything."

"So?"

"So I sent it back to get it fixed. I sent it to the main office and they fixed it. They had it about a week."

Frank nodded, remembering. "But it was okay when you got it back, right? It was all repaired."

"Yes. But it was gone a week, and that's the only time it's been out of my control. Somebody there must have done something to it."

"Maybe that guy you saw on the ship was involved somehow. Maybe . . ."

Frank was going to say that maybe the guy was an engineer or something and had learned how to alter the time chips. But before he could speak there was a singular blinding flash, like a thousand camera flashes going off, but all at one point. Now they were standing on a hill overlooking a series of cornfields. Below them a group of soldiers dressed in blue uniforms rode up on horses and pointed first at the top of the hill and then at a long line of men dressed in gray uniforms marching toward them on a dusty road.

"I've seen this before in history holograms," Frank said. "This is Gettysburg. Right before the battle. Those are Union troops pointing at us. And those others are Confederates coming to battle. We're in a bad place." There was a series of puffs of smoke from the men in blue, and half a second later the grass at the boys' feet was snipped by bullets zipping by. "A really bad place."

"And we're not alone." Dorso pointed to a small gnarled oak forty yards away. Behind the tree was the same man who had stood on the deck of the ship. He was blond and thin and Dorso could now see that he was probably in his early twenties. He was smiling a tight, thin, angry smile, and he yelled at them at the same moment that a booming sound came from below and cannons drowned out his voice.

"What? What did he say?" Dorso turned to Frank. But Frank wasn't there, he was down on his back, his eyes rolled up to show the whites, and there was a streak of blood on the side of his head. Dorso thought, He's been shot! Then there was another blinding flash and he was back by his locker. Frank was on the floor and there was still blood, real blood, on his head, and his eyelids were fluttering and then his eyes rolled back into focus. "What hap— Ow!"

Dorso sank down in relief. "Frank, Frank," he said. He was shaking. "You were shot at Gettysburg." He helped Frank sit up straight. "That guy yelled at us and when I turned you were down. You have blood on your head. Here." Dorso reached into his locker and took out a box of tissue. "It's a small cut. A bullet grazed you, I guess. But I thought . . . you were dead." His face felt clammy.

"Wait." Frank held up his hand. "You have tissue in your locker? What kind of guy has tissue in his locker?"

"The kind who finds dead bodies there." Dorso sighed. "I'd keep a garden hose if there was a place to attach it."

"What happened to you?" They turned to see Olivia Whelms holding her books and looking at Frank's head. Olivia never really listened to what anybody said and always spoke so that at least one word in every sentence was emphasized, but she almost never stressed the right word. "You *have* blood all over your head."

"I was shot," Frank said. "At Gettysburg. Right in the head. It was a grazing wound."

"Which *will* teach you not to open your locker so fast without moving your head *away*."

She moved off down the hall and Frank watched her go, shrugging. "If a truck hit her she wouldn't know it."

"He yelled something," Dorso said. "The guy was there, by that tree, just before you got hit, and he yelled something at us. I couldn't make it out."

"Oh, yeah." Frank nodded, then winced. "It was something about a combination. Like a snotty question or something. Like 'So you have the combination,' or 'How do you have it' or 'So you think you know the combination' or 'code' or 'sequence' . . ."

"Combination? Code?"

"I think so. Then I lost it. I got shot in the head, you know."

"Yes, I know."

"At Gettysburg."

"Yes. I know."

"Because of your laptop. So in a way I guess you could say I took a bullet for you."

Dorso ignored him. "Combination," he mused. "What did he mean by that?"

Frank dabbed at his head and saw that the bleeding had stopped. "I wonder if I should go to the school nurse. No. All those reports and things. How could I explain getting shot in the head at Gettysburg? And if I lied and said I'd hit my head on the locker like Olivia thinks, they'd want to come and inspect the locker. . . . I'll just let it go. I think he meant code."

"What? What did you say?"

"Code. Maybe there's some kind of combination or entry code that lets you into the time line or something."

Dorso stared at him. "That's it! A code. Let's say they did something to my computer when I sent it in to the factory and then put in a code to access the time line thing. You thought of that?"

Frank nodded. "It's all in here"—he tapped his temple softly—"just whizzing around. I think the bullet I took for you loosened up my thinking."

"You'll have to get shot more often."

Frank shook his head. "Another inch to the right and even Olivia wouldn't have blamed it on a locker."

"One more question: Why? Why do this to my laptop?"

Frank smiled. "The only thing I can think of is that it's a government conspiracy and cover-up centered on all the aliens from spaceships that landed back in the fifties and launched weather balloons to cover their tracks so they could hide and abduct people and examine their navels with a long copper wire."

"Frank."

"Or . . ."

"Or what?"

"Or it was a mistake. Somehow your laptop got a change that was meant for somebody else. In either case it means the same thing for us."

"What?"

"We have to break the code."

CHAPTER TEN

But for the moment they had to set the code aside, or try to. Frank went ahead and flunked the math test, which, considering that they were allowed to use their laptops as calculators, took some serious doing. It was only by playing hard on the pity note about his head, showing the cut his locker had given him, that he avoided the dreaded e-note of concern that otherwise would have been sent directly to his parents. Instead he won the right to take the test over the following week when his head was better.

Frank's parents had but one disciplinary procedure. If they got such a note he would be grounded until the situation was fixed, even if, as his father had said several times, that meant staying in and doing schoolwork until he was thirty and had his own family with boys to ground.

Dorso had his own problems.

He passed the math test but then wound up in biology lab partnered with Karen Bemis to dissect a virtual/cybernetic frog. Usually that would have been fine. He welcomed any chance to spend time with Karen. And she smiled at him and it looked like he might actually make a little headway on the Karen Bemis front . . .

Except.

As he went to the storage cupboard to pick up their virtual/cybernetic frog he carried his laptop—he was afraid to leave it near any other person alone—and there was a flash of light.

He found himself in thick jungle, waist deep in swamp water and almost solid mud.

"How did you get into our game?"

Next to him, sitting on a stump sticking out of the water, was the blond man. He had sharp features, a wisp of a lip beard and eyes that were green and seemed too bright, almost a hot green. Maybe a crazy green.

"What? Who? I mean what game?"

"How did you find out? Who told you? Was it Faron? I'll bet it was. Man, when I catch up with him I'll kill him. He's going to ruin it all, bringing in another person. It's just because he got bored, you know. He wanted to pick things up. But I don't see how you got a chip. . . . Come on, was it Faron who told you how to jump with my line?"

Dorso studied him. A second ago he had been reaching for a virtual/cybernetic frog, thinking of Karen Bemis, and now . . . and now what? "Who are you and what does all this mean?"

The man cocked his head, then smiled. "Man, you *don't* know, do you? I mean, this is all just happening to you and you don't have a clue. . . ." He threw back his head and laughed but there was no humor in it. A harsh laugh. "You don't know what you've gotten into at all, do you?"

"I know you're messing with the time paradox."

"You don't know anything at all. You got one of the chips by accident, or maybe not by accident, and you don't have a single idea of what's going on, do you? Man this is rich, really rich. Wait until I tell Faron."

A hissing growl seemed to come from the earth, low and deep and very, very close.

"What was that?" Dorso looked around at the water.

"Probably a crocodile. Of course, it's prehistoric and might be forty feet long, but they looked about the same then, or now, as they did in the future. Oh, there he is—see? He's big, but he looks just like a modern croc."

Dorso turned to see an enormous crocodile coming at him, not twenty yards away, its mouth slightly open.

"Man," the guy said. "Look at those teeth. Aren't they wild?"

The crocodile opened his mouth wide enough to easily swallow Dorso whole, and Dorso closed his eyes and waited for the crunch.

It never came. There was another flash and he was back in the biology lab, standing in front of the storage cabinet, hand still reaching for the frog. Except that he was soaked with mud and water from the waist down. He took the frog back to the table and put it down in front of Karen.

"What"—she looked at his pants—"happened to you?"

He looked down, then back up at her, knowing that it was over, that nothing he could ever say would make her forget how he looked at this moment. He said: "I had an accident."

She nodded. "I see that. You know . . ." Her eyes were

kind, and worse—far worse—full of pity. "You can get treatment for this kind of thing."

"Thank you." Dorso sighed. "I'm going to go to the bathroom now. To clean up."

"Yes. That would be a good idea. I'll wait to cut the frog until you get back."

"Thank you."

CHAPTER ELEVEN

"So it's a game." Frank nodded. "I thought as much."

They were back at Dorso's house so Dorso could watch Darling, who was dressing the cat as an astronaut. Dorso had told Frank about meeting the man in the prehistoric swamp. The cat, Dorso thought, looked catatonic. He smiled, wondering if that was where the word came from; somebody, somewhere, kept dressing a cat in different costumes until it simply sat there, numb. Darling was hooking the cat into a little parachute harness while she studied the upper landing of the staircase, and Dorso knew he would have to step in soon or the cat would be learning what free fall meant. "You didn't think any such thing."

"Well, maybe not, but I had a hunch." Frank smiled.

"Right." Dorso rubbed the back of his neck. He had started to have a dull ache back there about the time he'd shown up with wet pants in front of Karen. It wasn't getting worse, but it wasn't getting better either. Just a dull, throbbing ache. "The guy looked like one of those outlaw gamesters you see in the backs of magazines; kind of wild and crazy."

"So if it's a game, what kind of game is it?"

"A very dangerous one, if they're messing around with the time paradox. Remember last year when you went onto the Net and asked what would happen if you fundamentally changed the line of time, changed how things happened, so that you could actually go back and kill your own grandfather, which meant you wouldn't exist in the first place to go back and kill your grandfather, but if you did it then clearly you must exist even though if you didn't have a grandfather you couldn't exist to kill your own grandfather . . ." This, Dorso thought, isn't helping my neckache. "What did that theoretical physics professor tell you?"

"He said that time is based in some ways on the speed of light, and that if you alter time in an impossible way it's like trying to change the speed of light, which can't be done, and that in the end it can mean big trouble."

"How big?"

"Well, if you go back in time and you meet yourself and try to occupy the same place at the same time, it's apparently like bringing matter and antimatter together. Everything ends, ceases to exist."

"So that's their game? To make everything end? Are they that crazy?"

"Maybe, maybe not. Maybe it's just the gamester thing, you know. One guy does something, the next one tries to undo it, or fight it, or change it. But how did it all start?"

"He said something about a chip, a game chip, how he thought there were only two of them, and that I must have a third one. And he said something about how I jumped with his line. None of it made any sense until he mentioned that bit about it being a game."

Frank leaned back and closed his eyes, thinking, and Dorso smiled. When it was all done and you took away the joking and the constant search for nude women in history, Frank had a great brain and was really good at problem solving.

"Here's what I see," Frank said after a moment. "Somebody, somewhere, doctored a chip or a circuit in some way so as to allow it to alter the time paradox when it's put in a computer."

"Call it a hacker," Dorso said, walking across and taking the parachute harness off the cat when Darling was halfway up the staircase, cat hanging at her side. "A time hacker."

"Good one." Frank nodded. "All right. So not a scientist but a hacker stumbles onto a way to make a chip that cheats the time paradox. And then, instead of turning it over to the authorities, this hacker—let's call it hackers, more than one, because there had to be more than one to make the game concept work—so these hackers, instead of letting science know they've made this major breakthrough, wire it into their computers and set out to make it into some kind of game."

Dorso nodded and put the parachute on top of a bookcase so Darling couldn't get it. She went off holding the cat upside down. "A game where the result, if they're not careful, is the destruction of everything."

"The universe."

"And we know they did it at the factory," Dorso said. "Because somehow they put a chip in my computer by mistake when I sent it in to get it fixed. And apparently the chip was a duplicate of the one used by the blond guy because whenever he activates it, or whatever he does, it pulls my laptop and whoever is close to my laptop in with him."

"So if we use just the simplest form of detective work we can say that whoever did this has access to computers at the factory level. . . ."

"Might work at the factory."

"Right." Frank nodded. "At least one of them must work there. Maybe it was complicated enough that they couldn't do it anywhere except at the factory."

"So all we've got to do is go to the authorities and tell them what we've learned and they can track these guys down and stop them."

"Alll . . . riiight." Frank nodded again. "That's one *possible* solution."

"No." Dorso held his hand up toward Frank, which had the added benefit of stopping Darling, who was busy trying to stuff the cat tail first into a sock. "Not this time. I know where you're going with this, and we're not doing it."

"Where?" Frank said innocently.

"You're going to say we should jump into the game and track them down and stop them ourselves."

Frank frowned. "I wasn't going to say that exactly. I was going to say that seeing as how we've been involved with this since inception . . ."

" 'Inception'? You use a word like 'inception'?"

". . . seeing as how we've been involved since the *beginning*, we might be more qualified, might be the *most* qualified, if you will, to pursue these maniacs through time, beat them at their own game and thereby save the universe."

Dorso stared at him. "Have you been doing something to rattle your brain other than taking that bullet at Gettysburg?"

"Why?"

" 'Pursue these maniacs through time . . . and save the universe?' Are you listening to yourself?"

"Dorso, Dorso, Dorso . . ." Frank shook his head. "You're not seeing the whole picture."

"*I'm* not?"

"Look at it like it really is. These guys can really destroy the whole universe, we know what they're doing, maybe we can stop them. Right?"

"Unless, you know, we make a mistake." Dorso almost laughed. "And of course we *never* make mistakes."

"Name one, just one. You know, of this size. You know, a really big mistake . . ."

"Last Fourth of July. You tried to make a linear accelerator out of old car batteries and some ball bearings to see if you could shift the time holograms and see Nefertiti in her bath."

"So it didn't work. I'm not sure if it matters. When I saw Nefertiti with her clothes on she didn't look all that nice. Of course, it was hard to tell with all that makeup."

"Your accelerator took the back wall of the Halmers' garage off and went through the rear of Jung's Pretty Pastry Bakery so fast it detonated four racks of éclairs. If that ball bearing had hit somebody it would have vaporized them."

"Minor setbacks. As you said, nobody was hurt, and the insurance covered the reconstruction."

"Just the same, we are not going to play this game. Not this time. We are going to go to the authorities and tell them what's happening and let them handle these crazy gamesters and that's the end of it."

For a second Frank started to say something, but Dorso had that iron look in his eye, the look he got when there was just no changing his mind.

Oh, they went to the authorities and at first it was the same old story.

A bored time security officer sitting at a tired metal desk took down their names, or took down Dorso's name—they already had a file on Frank from his many attempts to circumvent the morality blocks—and then leaned back and sipped cold coffee and said:

"So what's the problem this time?"

Dorso took a breath. "Somebody, we think extreme gamesters, put a new kind of chip in my laptop and it allows them to cheat the time paradox and go back and affect things. You know, not just see them or bring them forward in holograms but actually go back and touch them, change them."

The officer closed his eyes, opened them. He pushed his notebook away and put his pencil down and sighed. "Right. How did you find this out?"

"Well, I saw Custer and he saw me, and then Beethoven, and then we ran into a mammoth, and then we were sent on a pirate ship . . ."

The security officer closed his eyes again, then looked at

Frank. "Is this some kind of trick to get around the codes again? I remember that last bit where you tried to sneak through a side entrance into Marie Antoinette's dressing room by following a carpet cleaner into the palace."

Frank did not point out that the Marie Antoinette episode was not the last time he'd tried to cheat the codes, it was just the last time the authorities were aware of. "No. I promise."

"Right." The security man stood up. "We'll get right on this and call you back."

"No, really." Dorso held up his laptop and pushed it across the desk. "It's really happening. I swear."

There was a grinding, slashing, blinding flash during which Dorso just had time to hear Frank say "Big mistake, pushing the laptop over," and the three of them, the desk and a floor lamp were suddenly sitting and standing on top of a sand dune in what had to be the Sahara Desert because they were completely surrounded by bedouin tribesmen on horses brandishing gleaming swords and short curved bows, all of them screaming high attack songs, while below them on the giant dune were arrayed several hundred knights in armor. In defensive positions.

Many things happened very rapidly. Frank just had time to say, calmly and with some authority, "I'd guess one of the early Crusades and we're with a small European detachment that's about to be wiped out."

"What? Who?" The time security officer said. "How did we get here?"

"That's how *I* sounded." Dorso nodded. "In the swamp."

"But this can't be happening!"

"Duck!" Frank yelled. "They're shooting at us!" Several hundred of the bedouins saw the desk and the men appear and let loose a cloud of arrows. "Quick, behind the desk!"

Dorso and Frank dove for cover. The officer stood for another half a second before the boys could drag him down, and one of the arrows went through the loose part of his shirt.

Half a heartbeat later, the three of them were looking at each other behind the desk. Then Dorso saw the gamester down with the knights. The guy hit two keys on his board and there was another flash and they were back in the office exactly as before except that the desk was covered with bedouin arrows.

"Your desk," Frank remarked to the stunned security officer, who was pulling at the arrow in his shirt, "looks like a porcupine."

"This could have killed me!"

"Exactly," Dorso said. "I told you it was serious."

"But it can't be. They can't move things around like that."

"They can and do," Frank said. "And we've got to stop them and save the universe."

"The secret," Dorso said, "is in the laptop." He reached across the desk and took the laptop back. For that second he was more than five feet away from the officer and his desk, but standing next to Frank. Then there was another intense white flash and everything disappeared.

"Oh, great," he had time to say, "here we go again."

CHAPTER TWELVE

Everything was dark. Pitch-black. Gradually, Dorso's eyes became accustomed to the dark and he realized that (a) they were in a cave and (b) the light that was so faint came from a torch or torches somewhere around the corner.

Frank was standing next to him. Dorso could just make out his features as well as the fact that he was still holding one of the arrows that had been stuck in the desk.

"Where are we?" Frank asked.

"A cave."

"Duh."

"Let's go toward the light."

"Oh, man," Frank said, "that's what they always tell you *not* to do in scary movies. 'Don't go toward the light,' they say, 'Stay out of the light. . . .' "

But Dorso was already moving.

"Shouldn't we have a plan?" Frank whispered as he caught up. "You know, about what to do when we catch up with these guys?"

"I have one."

"Do you want to share it?"

"We grab the guy's laptop before he can hit the button

and we take it back to the authorities, if that security man is still there and not in an institution or something."

"Oh, well, as long as it's not too difficult. You know, just grab the laptop and run. And what do you think this game freak is going to be doing while we're grabbing the laptop?"

But Dorso had gone around a corner and stopped dead.

The light was brighter now, although still flickering and soft. They had entered a kind of chamber. It had a low, rounded ceiling, and three men, three naked, indescribably dirty men covered with facial and body hair, were holding torches and painting with brushes that seemed to be made of the ends of shredded twigs or perhaps stiff animal hair.

The paintings were of animals, what looked like deer or elk and perhaps a bison. They were graceful; even in the dim light they looked incredibly beautiful.

Prehistoric times, Dorso thought. We're in France when Cro-Magnon man was making the cave paintings.

The first recorded art. In all their time playing with holograms and seeing living history Dorso and Frank had never come to this moment. The first example of recorded art was being made.

It stunned him. There would be thousands of years of man's history and art to follow this moment, hundreds of centuries of art, with Michelangelo and Rembrandt and the Egyptian pyramids, and none of it was really any better than what these men were doing in the cave.

Even Frank was silent, and it was just as well because neither of them had been seen. The three men were focused intently on their painting, speaking in monosyllables.

The gamester was sitting on a small rock with his back to the boys not five feet away, staring up at the painters. He too seemed amazed. On his right knee lay his laptop.

It was Frank who had the presence of mind to step quietly forward, lean over and snatch the gamester's laptop from his knee. He jumped back into the darkness.

For an instant there was no reaction. Then the gamester turned and stood up. "What are you doing?"

"We're stopping you!" Dorso said. "Come on, Frank, let's go!"

"Where can you go?" The gamester didn't come after them. "There's nowhere to run and you don't know the escape codes."

"Wrong," Dorso said. "I saw you hit the keys to escape in the desert. Get close, Frank, we're leaving."

"Don't leave me here, not with them!"

The three painters had turned and were staring in shock at the apparition. Clothed, twenty-first century humans with sneakers and almost no body or facial hair? But their shock quickly gave way to something like anger and they came at the three time travelers.

Dorso had lied. Oh, he *had* seen the gamester hit the keys and get them out of the mess in the Crusades, but he hadn't seen exactly the right keys.

He knew the first one was F1 and he *thought* the second one was A, but it could have been S or Q or Z or even X or W. So he took a quick breath, leaned close to Frank, held down F1 and hit them all as fast as he could.

The effect was astonishing.

There was the same flash of white light and then they

proceeded on an encyclopedic dash through all the time periods they had entered so far. In the space of what seemed like a couple of seconds they went from the cave to the security man's office to the desert and back to the office to the swamp and back to the classroom with Karen to the pirate ship and back to the door of Dorso's home to the mammoth butt and back to the sidewalk in front of the library and the battlefield and then, finally, to what was apparently Kitty Hawk in 1903. Wilbur and Orville Wright were about to launch their flying machine for the first time.

"I think," Frank said, "I'm going to throw up. Everything is spinning."

"No." Dorso held his shoulder. "Over there, on the side of the hill, there's another gamester. What does he have? Is that some kind of weapon?"

The scene was below them. The flying machine was sitting on a track about twenty yards in front of and below where they were on the side of the hill. The gamester seemed to be aiming what looked like a gun but turned out to be a net-firing device used by naturalists to capture birds.

"It's a net gun," Frank said. "I've seen them used on the nature channels. He's going to fire that thing and knock the plane down!"

"That's the game," Dorso said. "I'll bet the game is one of them tries to change history, change the time line, and the other is supposed to stop him."

"But if they don't take off this time with the plane they'll just take off next time."

"Not necessarily. What if it wrecks and hurts one of the

Wright brothers? Or kills one of them? Then they won't invent the airplane."

The gamester with the net gun was off to the side, looking away from them. He waited for the Wrights and the man the brothers had asked to assist them by taking a picture as the plane glided into the air. They were all concentrating on the flying machine and didn't see the gamester or the boys. Dorso leapt forward and used his shoulder to knock the gamester down before he could fire. The gamester had rolled his laptop up and jammed it in a back pocket of his pants. When he fell it flew clear, but neither Dorso nor Frank saw it.

Instead, Dorso took his own laptop, and with Frank close and nearly lying on top of the gamester, he again hit F1 and all the nearby keys (he still didn't know which key did the job). He triggered the flash and the ripping ride through time again, taking the gamester and his laptop and the net gun with them.

"This time I'm *definitely* going to throw up," Frank said. "You have *got* to quit doing that. . . ."

"Get his laptop! Get his laptop!"

The gamester was astonished to find himself with two strangers and even more astonished to find himself in a stark desert, about to be run down by a stagecoach pulled by six lathered horses being whipped to a full gallop.

Native Americans were chasing the stagecoach. They had scruffy-looking horses and there seemed to be a dozen or so of them, apparently Apaches, all with guns, all shooting at the coach.

"Where are we?" Frank asked.

"His laptop! There, on the ground! Grab it!" Dorso was fairly screaming. "And the net gun. Grab everything!"

Frank came to his senses and dove for the laptop as Dorso rolled off the gamester and fell toward him. The stagecoach thundered past and clouds of dust covered them just as the Apaches rode up. Dorso hit the keys and they screamed through time again until they were at the present. Dorso took a breath and was about to run from the gamester, who had been brought along with them, when there was a kind of *whumph* of light. They fell further back in the past until the three, with Frank holding the gamester's laptop and Dorso holding the net gun, came to a stop in a dark alley in a very smoky city where a woman so covered in soot she seemed to be made of dirt looked at the three of them and said in a Cockney accent:

"Well, lookee 'ere, ducks, wot the cat's drug in. . . ."

The gamester made a move to grab the laptop. Dorso fired the net gun at him and wrapped him up. He shoved the tangled bundle over to the side of the alley, handing the loose ends of the net ropes to the woman. "Here, this is for you."

Then he turned to Frank and said, "I'm guessing London, in the eighteen-fifties—I recognize it from when I did that paper on Charles Dickens. Should we run and hide here until we can figure out how to work this time-jump business or just hit all the keys again and see where we come to?"

Frank threw up.

"Right." Dorso nodded. "We'll stay here a bit until we figure it out. Come on, let's get away from this geek before he gets loose."

And they ran off down the alley, leaving the woman holding the net and gamester as if she had a pig in a poke.

CHAPTER THIRTEEN

In the darkness of the back alleys of London, where the smog from the coal fires used for heating houses was so thick that daylight never really dawned, the boys quickly found themselves an alcove back in a building and squatted against the wall.

Dorso took a deep breath and coughed with the smog. He spit soot into the gutter. "Man, this is awful stuff."

Frank nodded. "You should try throwing up. The smog kind of mixes with the vomit and makes a really great taste."

"All right, all right. That's enough. Thank you for sharing."

Frank shrugged, wiping his mouth with his sleeve. "Just keeping you up to date."

"Right now I'm more interested in understanding how all this works."

"We have them both."

"What?"

"Two laptops. Didn't you say the gamester said there were two of them? We've got three now, yours and the two others. That's it. So what do we do now?"

Dorso shook his head. "The same thing applies as before. If we can get back to where we were, we go straight to the authorities and let them handle all this. They'll believe us now, or that one guy will, with his desk full of arrows. They can work the investigation backward and see how it all started."

"Right," Frank said, smiling. "That's what we'll do."

"You've got that tone in your voice."

"What tone?"

"That kind of smart-aleck sound you make when you think you know something I don't."

Frank shrugged. "It's just that you said we'd turn it over to the authorities, but then you went ahead and started busting the gamesters yourself."

"I didn't have any control over that. We just got caught up."

"So what's different now? We still don't know what keys to hit to get back to the present."

Dorso was quiet. Frank was right.

"I think we have to kill their laptops," Dorso said. "Shut them down."

Frank shook his head. "Not so fast. We don't know how this all works. Maybe we need their laptops to make the whole time-travel thing work. If we shut them down we might get stuck here. I mean, I like England, but I figure if I have to breathe this slop for more than a day or two I'll drop dead. We're not used to breathing pure smoke. Even in the bad smog cities it's not nearly this bad. . . ." He trailed off because Dorso was frowning, obviously thinking. "What's the matter?"

"I just thought of something else."

Frank waited. "Well?"

"Remember all those silly shows that used to be on television? About space and all the monsters and how they could go faster than light—I think they called it warp speed?"

"Sure. Sometimes they're still fun to watch. It's all so hokey."

"Well, they did this thing called transporting. . . ."

"Sure. Where they dematerialize in one place and then materialize in another. Like I said, it's all so hokey. They tried all that years ago and found that with the trillions of cells it takes to make you human, even if they could somehow dematerialize one of us and bring us back it probably wouldn't work. I mean, if just one cell was wrong, you'd wind up with a monster. Like that old movie about the guy who tried it and there was a fly in the chamber with him and he mixed with the fly and came out *all* messed up. Man, he was drinking milk with this kind of hairy nose thing that slobbered all over the place—"

"They're doing it with us."

"Doing what with us?"

"We're being transported somehow. Look, when we use our laptops to just view the past, the hologram comes forward. I mean, I've never figured out quite how it works, even when they tell us in class, because it's so complicated and involves all that speed-of-light stuff. But I know *we* don't move. The hologram comes to us, we don't go to it."

"And they're moving us somehow." Frank finished the thought for him.

"Exactly. I think they're transporting the viewer, us, in

some way because we don't just sit in one place and let it come to us. We're being sent everywhere—ancient France, Kitty Hawk, London, the Southwest deserts, northern Africa during the Crusades—we're getting dragged all *over* the place. And it's real, not just a hologram."

"They've learned how to transport people not just through time but space as well."

Dorso nodded. "This is big, really big. I mean, it was something when they cheated the time paradox and could affect time, but if they've really found a way to transport humans from one spot to another . . . oh, man—no more cars, not even the electrics we have now. No planes needed. None of it. This changes the whole world."

Frank held up his hand and then, realizing Dorso couldn't see it in the dark alcove, said, "Just a minute. If they could transport people, wouldn't they be doing just that? Maybe it only works when's it's used for time travel somehow."

"Maybe, but even so, they can still do it just for moving people and not have anything to really do with time travel. Just make it a minute in the past. Let's say we're in London, which we are, but it's present day, and we want to transport ourselves to our houses in the present. All we do is transport ourselves a minute into the past—"

"Or a second, or a half a second," Frank cut in. "A tenth of a second."

"Exactly. We go a tenth of a second in the past and bang, we're home and haven't lost any time. We've been transported, essentially, within the present."

"They've done it. They've figured out how to transport."

"And all *we've* got to do is figure it out and we can end this whole thing. Get back to the authorities and tell them that everything in the whole world is different now."

"Oh, wow. I just thought of something. If we can transport—"

Another blinding flash, even brighter in the darkness of the London smog.

"Dorso, you didn't have to do that!"

"It wasn't me!" Dorso just had time to yell. "It wasn't me! There's somebody else!"

CHAPTER FOURTEEN

This time they were in a room.

There was one electric light hanging from the ceiling, two wooden chairs and a wooden table. None of it looked very old or very new. The boys, and their laptops, arrived in the corner of the room furthest from the table.

There was a solid door with no glass in it, and there were no windows in the room, but to the left of the door a small speaker was mounted in the wall.

Frank stepped across to the door and tried the knob. "It's locked."

"I'm not surprised."

There was a rasping sound from the speaker. "Sit at the chairs by the table." The voice was not loud but low and modulated. Not human. Or perhaps human but spoken through a filter or scrambler or amplifier.

The boys stood for a few seconds without moving and the voice came on again.

"Sit *down*! If you do not, you will be relocated into a pool of water filled with piranhas."

"How can they see us?" Frank said.

"Microcameras," Dorso answered. "A tiny dot on the wall."

"You're very bright," the voice said. "Yes, we can see you, and hear you. Now sit down. It's for your comfort. We may be here for some time."

"We might as well." Dorso knelt and looked beneath the furniture. "I can't see anything wrong."

The boys moved to the chairs and sat at the table.

"How did you find the players?"

It was a strange voice, but it also seemed to have feeling.

"What do you mean?" Dorso asked.

"Don't be cute," the voice said. "You know what I'm talking about."

I'm, Dorso thought. It's a single person. Of course, he could be anywhere, or, Dorso thought, smiling, any*time*, but something about the voice made him think the person was nearby; almost as if he wanted to meet the boys, to come in and talk to them.

"I see the camera," Frank whispered without moving his lips. "Over the doorjamb. A dark spot."

The voice said nothing and Dorso answered the whisper in an even lower voice. "It's not a good mike. He can't hear us if we talk this low."

"So what do we do?"

"I repeat, how did you find the players?"

"It wasn't intentional," Dorso said aloud, then whispered to Frank, "Get up and move around so you're blocking me from the camera. Do it slowly, like you're examining the room."

Frank spoke low. "What are you doing?"

"I'm going to cut off all three laptops so he can't control us." Then, in a louder tone: "It was all a mistake. Somehow . . ."

Frank got up and stood to the side, looking at the table and then the wall, humming. When he was directly in front of Dorso he paused, looking up at the camera.

"Move away, move away from the door and back to your seat!"

Dorso had the three laptops rolled in his hand. He unrolled them, hit the pressure power pads on each, and cut them off. There, he thought, now we shall see what we shall see. "Come on," he whispered to Frank, "sit back down."

"Somehow," he went on loudly, "my laptop was modified to react to your signal. It was all an accident. And you're wrong, we really don't know what's happening. We just keep getting bounced around to all sorts of places without wanting to."

There was a pause; then, in an exasperated tone, the voice said, "You've turned off the computers."

"He tried," Dorso whispered to Frank. "He tried to time-jump us and it didn't work."

"So now what?"

"Now we wait," Dorso said softly.

"For what?"

"For the door to open," Dorso said. "I think he's close and he'll come in to get the laptops. Be ready to run."

But for a long time it seemed that Dorso was wrong.

There was nothing. No sound from the speaker, no movement at the door. The boys got up and moved around, stretched, whispered.

"Where do you think we are?" Frank asked.

"I think the question might be more *when* do I think we are," Dorso said. "But either way, I don't have a clue. The walls are drywall, there's electricity, the furniture is modern, so I'd guess we aren't too far in the past, but other than that, who knows? We could be anywhere in the world. I think I know one thing: for this guy to do any more damage to us he's got to get hold of these laptops, and to do *that* he's got to come in here."

He stopped. The knob on the door turned. The door began to swing open.

"Get ready," Dorso breathed. "Get ready to run."

When the door swung open it revealed Darling holding the cat.

"Darling?!" Dorso said. "What are *you* doing here?"

"Play cat," she said, smiling, looking at Dorso and yet somehow through him. "Play cat," and then there was a hiss and a glimmer of light. Smiling, she said, "Play cat . . ."

"It's a trick, a hologram!" Frank yelled. "Jump through it. *Move!*" With the yell he practically climbed Dorso's back and drove him through the door . . .

. . . into what looked like Dorso's living room, with his mother standing there.

"Mom?"

"It's another hologram. Keep moving, past the blurry edge, run!"

But Dorso was with him now, knew it was all fake, and he dove through his mother's image, through the replica of his living room, then his own room, then a hologram of his bicycle (My *bicycle?* he thought), then a montage of blurry images of everything from Custer to Beethoven to his locker and cadavers and finally a wall, with another door, and they piled through *that* door to find themselves not in a living room but a garage, a plain old garage on the side of a house that had been turned into a workshop. There, at a high work chair by a workbench, sat what Dorso could only think of as the perfect 1990s computer geek: a thin, semibald man of about forty with a pocket protector in his shirt pocket full of pens (nobody used pens anymore; very few people wrote at all except electronically). He had thick glasses (nobody wore glasses anymore, since they had corrective eye surgery). On the bench in front of him was a laptop.

"Wait a minute!" Frank stopped dead. "*You're* the game master? You look like Elmer Fudd from those old cartoons!"

But Dorso was moving too fast to stop and he hit the man full on, knocking him sideways. The chair went down with the man on top of it. He had grabbed at his laptop on the way down and held one side of it with Dorso catching the other, his own three laptops flying off into a pile in the corner near where Frank stood.

There was a beat when everything seemed to stop. Frank stood, the man lay on the floor with his laptop in his hand, Dorso on top of him holding the other side of the laptop, the keyboard twisted. Then the man looked at him and smiled a sad little smile and said in a soft voice, "Thank you, and goodbye." Then he pushed Dorso five or six feet away and hit F1 and WS on the keyboard. There was a brief flash of light—though not nearly as intense as before—and he was gone.

Dorso and Frank were still there in the workshop, but the man was gone.

"Man," Frank said, "you almost had that laptop!"

Some seconds passed while Dorso thought about what had just happened. Then he stood and brushed his knees where they had ground into the dirty garage floor. "He's gone."

"I know. I saw him vanish."

"No. I saw his eyes. Something was there, something . . . not quite right. The way he smiled and said 'Thank you, and goodbye.' Like he was really sad. I think he's gone, and what's more—"

He was interrupted by a rustling in the corner where he'd thrown the three laptops. As he and Frank watched there was a blur of light and a wiggle and the two captured laptops vanished. Dorso's, which had been resting on top of them, dropped an inch to the floor.

"I mean, he's gone."

"Where?"

"It will be like he was never here. The chip in my computer is gone, all of the images, the changes in time are gone."

"I'll bet he went back," Frank said, "and killed his grandfather."

"Maybe. Something like that. Maybe. Heck, *I* don't know. Nothing like this has ever happened before—how could anybody know?"

"But if he's gone, I mean, like he really wasn't there to

begin with, then how come we still know about him? How can he be in our memories . . ." Frank trailed off. "I just had a really bad thought."

Dorso smiled, a small smile not unlike the one the man had given him. "Just one? I've had about four hundred, and that's just in the last three or four minutes. Like how about all the good that could have been done instead of just a game and all the silly pranks? We could have saved Lincoln, saved JFK, could have maybe ended wars before they began, stopped the plague—"

"Where are we?" Frank cut in. "Not just when, but where? With that whole transporter thing we could be any-where in the world."

"I think I know, but let's step outside to make sure."

They went to the side door in the garage. Dorso opened it and they moved out into a bright, sunshiny day. Birds were singing, small clouds moved serenely across a blue sky, and before they had taken two steps Frank yelped.

"We're on Fourth Street! There's Anderson's Funeral Parlor. . . ."

Dorso nodded. "And more to the point, we're in the present. He just used this garage as a place to meet us. It's not really his workshop. He doesn't live here. It was just a place to bring us so he could get the laptops."

"But he didn't need to," Frank said. "All he had to do was go back in time and make them not happen."

"Right," Dorso said, smiling. "I'd forgotten that." He sighed, tired now—exhausted—but more too: sad. Why, he thought, am I sad? "Maybe he just wanted to meet us."

"Sure. Man cheats time, makes a game of destroying the

universe and then wants to meet a couple of podunk kids from a small town. Happens all the time. I'll tell you what I think, I think he's vanished in time and we'll never see him again, and I'm glad it's that way. He scared me half to death with those eyes and pens and pocket protector. I mean, you don't know *what* he might do."

"I don't know. I'd like to meet him again. There was something in his eyes that I kind of liked. But I suppose you're right—we'll never hear from him again."

But this time Frank was wrong.

CHAPTER FIFTEEN

Weeks passed, then months, and at first there was some investigating because the time security officer remembered that he had jumped through time and a whole bunch of people had shot his desk full of arrows and then the arrows had strangely disappeared. But there was no odd chip in Dorso's computer, and the factory had no indication of anything strange happening, and there was no sign anywhere of the little man with the pocket protector and the ballpoint pens.

In time the security man's memory faded and when there was no evidence and no further strange happenings even Dorso and Frank stopped talking about it.

Frank went back to trying to cheat the morality blocks and had some success; he was fairly certain he had seen Helen of Troy's bare upper arm and elbow, or it might have been a knee. Dorso finally worked up the courage to ask Karen Bemis to go to a movie and to his immense shock and surprise she accepted—this was after he had taken some time to explain that he didn't have a "problem" but that the faucet near the materials closet had sprayed him on the way by.

The date, if it could be called that, went off almost without a hitch, except that Dorso was so afraid of saying the wrong thing that he nearly didn't talk at all and later had absolutely no idea what the movie was about, even though it had been fully interactive with motion, sound, smell and taste.

He walked her home in a daze and she kissed him on the cheek, which further unnerved him, so that he walked nearly another block before he realized that his laptop, which was rolled up in his back pocket, was insistently signaling that he had an urgent message.

The message was anonymous. It said:

"Please go look under your front porch."

That was it. It could have been a prank, but he knew it wasn't Frank because Frank could not resist using his icon—an outline of a nude—when he sent e-mail. He didn't know anybody else well enough for a practical joke.

Under your porch . . .

And he knew. He did not know how he knew, but he was certain the message was from the time hacker. Nor was he afraid. He didn't know why, but nothing about the circumstance frightened him. This was a request and he hurried home to comply.

Dorso's house was old-fashioned and had a lattice around the underside of the front porch that half hid the space beneath it. Darling played there often, in the cool darkness, because the cat kept trying to hide there and she chased him wherever he went.

There was an opening near the right side and Dorso

crouched and worked his way through. There on the ground, glowing slightly, sat a laptop. Above the keyboard on the screen was the message:

"Hit F1WS while holding the computer."

And Dorso did it without hesitating. Much later, he considered it and realized that nothing in the world could have kept him from hitting the keys.

There was a flash of light, though controlled and subdued, and Dorso found himself standing under a giant oak tree in a thick forest on a summer afternoon. Sitting on a log nearby was the hacker.

"Hello," he said. "Glad you could make it. When I had that chip in your computer I could tell where you were but now I just had to use the regular computer systems. . . . It's very frustrating."

"I see you're back at it, playing with time," Dorso said. "Moving me around."

The man laughed, though not unkindly. "Not this time. Or not so much. Where we're standing is where your front porch will be in two hundred years, nine months and sixteen days. We moved in time but not space."

"I would like," Dorso said carefully, "for you to tell me just what's been going on. If you would. Please."

The hacker nodded. "That's why I called you. I had hoped that your friend would be with you because the two of you really saved my life and I wanted to thank you both. But without that chip I couldn't tell anything about you or if he was with you. You can explain to him later."

"Explain what?"

"Exactly." The man laughed. "Tell him exactly what . . ." He paused and watched a bird fly past and Dorso realized that the forest around them was alive with the sounds of birds singing. "Don't you think this is much nicer than a housing development?" the man asked, but Dorso could tell he didn't really expect an answer because he was thinking. "How to start . . . Well, here, let's do it this way. I am an engineer and I made some fundamental discoveries that will change how we think about everything forever. How's that?" He smiled at Dorso.

"Too quick. How come you're the only one who did this, who understood this?"

The man looked at the trees again, then nodded. "A good question. Sometimes the most amazing discoveries are made by one person who has a bit of luck. Madame Curie discovered radiation—and it killed her later because she didn't know how deadly it could be. One man in a Texas garage discovered that silicon would let current flow only one way, and that led to transistors, which led to chips . . . well, you get my drift. One day I was sitting in the lab—I worked for the computer company that makes your laptop—and I remembered that many years ago a man named Michelson discovered that light, the photons of light, have mass. I theorized that if images are made of light, which has mass, and can be moved through time and space—as we have been doing with historical holograms—then why not the bigger mass, the actual person or thing. I worked to develop a chip that would incorporate my thinking, or several chips working together, and one day I sent a banana from my lunch back ten minutes. Then a week later I sent my cat, Richard, back a day with no ill effects. The following week I sent myself back a month."

"And nobody at the company knew you were doing this?"

"Correct. I kept it secret for two reasons. One, it would make a devastatingly destructive weapon in the wrong hands, and I am a peace-loving man."

"And the second reason?" Dorso almost smiled, thinking of Frank and his always having two reasons.

"That's a bit more complicated. Part of it is that I have always been poor and do not believe in wealth, but with this discovery, I am ashamed to admit that I started to think in terms of personal gain. And the other part is pure ego. I had made a stupendously colossal discovery that could change the world, and if I let it out it would no longer be just my discovery."

"And it got out," Dorso said. "The two gamesters found out what you were doing."

"Precisely. I was not as secure as I thought. One of them hacked into my computer when I was online gathering some of the initial data on how Michelson discovered the mass of light. Eventually they got my address through further hacking and the two of them showed up at my door. They took my computer by force, and two extra chips that I had been working on, and told me I had to continue to keep it all a secret or they would destroy me and the rest of the world."

"And you believed them?"

"Not at first. But you saw them, you saw their eyes! Then they started playing that game about one trying to change time while the other one tried to stop him, playing a game that could literally end everything, and I realized they were telling the truth. They would do anything."

"Why didn't you go to the authorities?"

"It was impossible. The hackers could act faster than me, and although I manufactured two more chips without them knowing about it, they would know if I tried anything. They also worked at the company and watched me like a hawk, both digitally and on camera. There was nothing I could do. So I worked out a kind of plan—a thought, really—that if I could somehow get somebody else involved maybe that person could do something."

"Why me?"

"Why not? They wouldn't suspect you, you're young, you seemed to be bright, judging by your work on the computer—I looked in the memory when I worked on it. And there was the time issue. I was running out of it, to be blunt. They were starting to play dumber and dumber tricks on each other, and it was just a matter of time . . . I guess it wasn't much of a plan"—he smiled again—"but as you can see, it worked."

"Why the pranks? The bodies, the worms . . . all of it?"

Here he laughed. "The chips are not static. They learn by doing. Initially they were not complete but had to learn to make the jumps through time. I did some of the pranks just to get the chips started, and then they did more of their own pranks while they learned. When they locked in—I believe it was the first time you saw Custer looking at you—I knew they were close and I stopped the pranks. In the beginning they keyed to the same points in time and space as one of the—what did you call them, the gamesters?—but as they learned, they would go anywhere any of the other chips would go."

"We could have been hurt or killed!" Dorso said. "We were in danger, attacked—arrows were shot at us."

"We could all have been killed. We probably *would* have all been killed if it hadn't have been for you and your friend."

"Frank."

"Yes. Frank. I tried to help but I couldn't do much. . . ."

"What about at the end? What was all that in the room in the garage and the holograms of my sister and my mother and my bicycle?"

"I thought . . . well, perhaps I *didn't* think as much as I should have, but I had a small hope that once it was all over perhaps I could somehow get your laptop back without you knowing who I am or what really had happened. I was wrong."

"Why not just do what you finally did do? Just go back and erase the chip and everything? That's what finally happened anyway. In fact, why didn't you just do that in the first place?"

"Once they started watching me I couldn't really do anything overtly, and before that there wasn't really a problem, was there?"

Dorso thought about it, or thought as much as his

whirling brain would let him. There were still a thousand questions he wanted to ask, and he wished Frank was there to help him.

"I know it all seems confusing."

"Confusing is a good word," Dorso said. "Another one is insane, as in am I going insane?"

He laughed. "No."

"So why did you come back? Why did you come to see me?"

"Because you helped me so much by getting the computers away from those two. I thought I owed you some kind of explanation, and then too I thought I owed you something for all your trouble. As you said, you could have been killed."

"So what now?"

"Now I will leave and I will spend the rest of my life moving through and studying time, and making certain that if this is ever rediscovered it will only be used for good purposes."

"What about me? And Frank? And the gamesters?"

"Ah, yes. Well, as for the gamesters, they're doing surprisingly well. The one in Victorian London has struck up quite a friendship with the young lady you left him with— her name is Lily, by the way—and the one in the cave, well, let's just say that Cro-Magnon man is more compassionate than I thought, and he has joined one of their clans. As for you boys, as I said, I thought I owed you something. Soo . . ." The man suddenly looked up. "Oh, look, a flight of passenger pigeons—white men hunted them to extinction, you know. Aren't they beautiful?"

Dorso watched the enormous flock of birds as they wheeled over the clearing and disappeared. There must have been ten or fifteen thousand of them.

"They used to darken the sky." The hacker looked after the birds.

Dorso waited. Then: "You were saying about Frank and me . . ."

"Oh, yes. Well, in a moment you'll hit F1WS on the laptop and that will take you back to beneath your porch in the present. About twenty seconds after you arrive the laptop will disappear. You will then go to Frank's house and get him and come back to your yard, and about three feet from the northeast corner of your garage you will instruct Frank to kick the ground several times, whereupon you will discover a small, half-rotted wooden chest buried in a shallow hole."

"What's in it?"

"Confederate gold coins that a small group of men were taking west in the last year of the Civil War to start a small army in Mexico. They were waylaid by bandits and all of the men on both sides were either killed right there or died of their wounds a short time later. It's important that Frank discover it because he gets half of the gold, and that way your parents won't object because it's on your land."

"Did you . . . I mean, were you . . . I guess I want to know how those men died."

"I see. No, I didn't hurt them. As I told you, I hate violence. They killed each other. All I did was move the gold from where they initially buried it, which is now under a freeway overpass seven miles south of town. I promise."

"You talk like this is a lot of gold."

"Well, I guess that depends on what you consider a lot. By some standards it's not so much, but it should put you through college, both of you, and your sister and Frank's brothers and sisters, and set you up in business if that's what you want. In today's market, with gold better than forty-four hundred dollars an ounce or about seventy thousand dollars a pound . . ."

"How heavy is it?"

"Just a hair over thirty pounds. I'd guess it's worth a little over two million dollars. Of course, there will be taxes and all. Still, you should be comfortable."

"Two million dollars . . . comfortable. You call that comfortable?"

He nodded. "Like Frank said, you saved the universe. It's the least I can do. Now hit F1WS or we'll be here all day."

"Will I see you again?"

A long pause. "I don't think so. But there's a slight chance. I've started to work on extrapolating time predictions, moving the mass ahead of the moment."

"Seeing into the future? But they said it couldn't be done because it hasn't happened yet."

"And it can't. Yet. But we can see down a road before we walk down it, can't we? And I was looking down your time road recently. You have a very interesting life ahead of you, from what I can see."

"If you can see what's coming I have a question."

"No. Not yet, maybe not ever. Now hit the keys and go get Frank. You have a lot to do."

And Dorso hit the keys. He rode the flash of light and was back under his porch and then out walking to get Frank, who was about to have a very good day, before he realized that he still didn't have an answer to the one question that was really bothering him.

Would Karen Bemis go out with him again?

About the Author

Gary Paulsen is the distinguished author of many critically acclaimed books for young people, including three Newbery Honor books: *The Winter Room, Hatchet* and *Dogsong*. His novel *The Haymeadow* received the Western Writers of America Golden Spur Award. Among his Random House books are *Molly McGinty Has a Really Good Day*; *The Quilt* (a companion to *Alida's Song* and *The Cookcamp*); *The Glass Café*; *How Angel Peterson Got His Name*; *Caught by the Sea: My Life on Boats*; *Guts: The True Stories Behind* Hatchet *and the Brian Books*; *The Beet Fields*; *Soldier's Heart*; *Brian's Winter, Brian's Return* and *Brian's Hunt* (companions to *Hatchet*); *Father Water, Mother Woods*; and five books about Francis Tucket's adventures in the Old West. Gary Paulsen has also published fiction and nonfiction for adults, as well as picture books illustrated by his wife, the painter Ruth Wright Paulsen. Their most recent book is *Canoe Days*. The Paulsens live in New Mexico and on the Pacific Ocean.